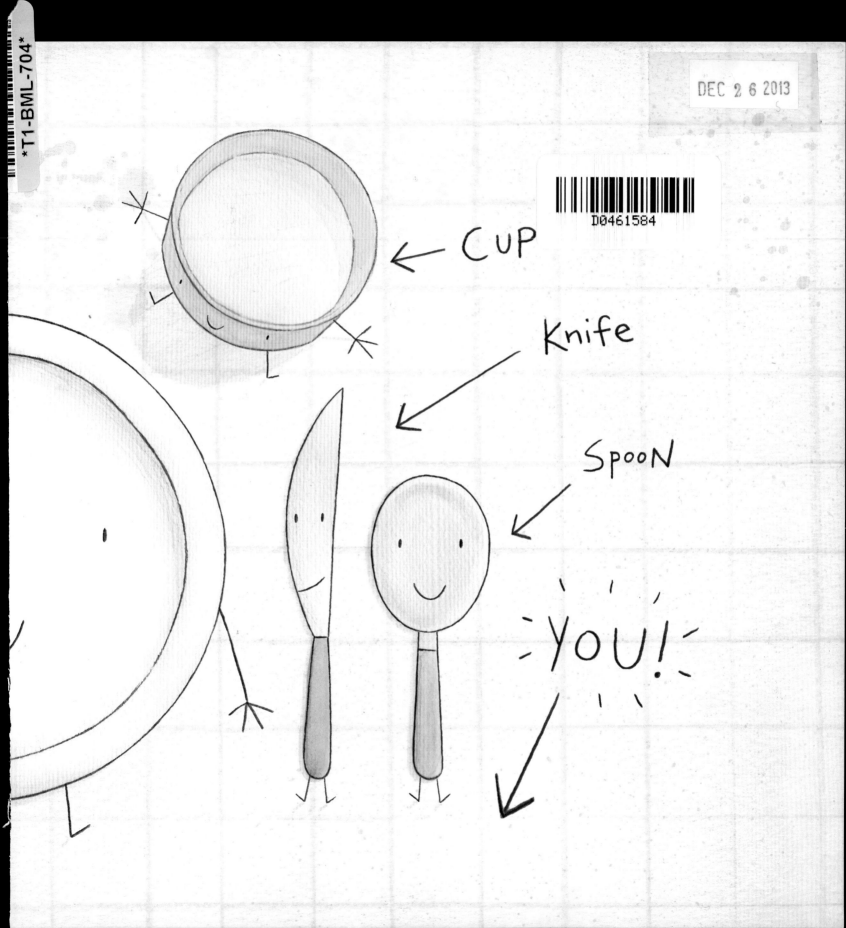

For my sister, Samantha—
it's your turn to set the table

First published in the United States of America in September 2013
by Walker Books for Young Readers, an imprint of Bloomsbury Publishing, Inc.
www.bloomsbury.com

For information about permission to reproduce selections from this book, write to
Permissions, Walker BFYR, 1385 Broadway, New York, New York 10018
Bloomsbury books may be purchased for business or promotional use. For information on bulk purchases
please contact Macmillan Corporate and Premium Sales Department at specialmarkets@macmillan.com

Library of Congress Cataloging-in-Publication Data
Clanton, Ben, author, illustrator.
The table sets itself / by Ben Clanton.
pages   cm
Summary: Setting the table turns from a giant bore to an exciting chore for young Izzy.
ISBN 978-0-8027-3447-1 (hardcover) · ISBN 978-0-8027-3448-8 (reinforced)
[1. Table setting and decoration–Fiction. 2. Chores–Fiction. 3. Youths' art.] I. Title.
PZ7.C52923Tab 2013   [E]–dc23   2013007475

Art created with HB pencils, watercolors, paper textures, and Adobe Photoshop
Typeset in Monroe Light
Book design by Nicole Gastonguay

Printed in China by C&C Offset Printing Co., Ltd., Shenzhen, Guangdong
1 3 5 7 9 10 8 6 4 2 (hardcover)
1 3 5 7 9 10 8 6 4 2 (reinforced)

THE TABLE SETS ITSELF

Ben Clanton

WALKER BOOKS FOR YOUNG READERS
AN IMPRINT OF BLOOMSBURY
NEW YORK   LONDON   NEW DELHI   SYDNEY

Izzy and her friends Dish, Fork, Knife, Spoon, Cup, and Napkin had waited for what felt like a bigillion years to set the table themselves.

So when Mom finally asked Izzy to help for the first time, they all set to it straightaway.

Woo-hoo!

Wee Woo

Dish, front and center, please.
Cup, you go here.

They did such a good job that Mom had them set the table the next night and the next night.

After being stuck in the same old places for what must have been a zillion times, Izzy and her friends were fed up.

THIS IS SO BBORRINGG!!!

We should ALL change spots.

Everyone agreed that switching places was the best idea since macaroni and cheese, and they started trying all sorts of new table settings!

Some of them were recipes for disaster.

But eventually
they all settled
on spots they liked.

Izzy and her friends loved their new spots on the table, but Izzy's parents didn't understand.

"Little girls sit on chairs," said Dad.

"Back to your proper spot NOW," said Mom.

Everyone went back to their old places. Nobody
was happy, but Dish and Spoon were especially
sour. They had REALLY liked being next to
each other, dishing out the latest scoop, so . . .

. . . Dish ran away with Spoon.

The next day at breakfast, Dish and Spoon still hadn't returned. No other plate or spoon would do, and Izzy was getting hungry . . .

Too LONG

Too *fancy*

Too **squarish**

They looked EVERYWHERE for Dish and Spoon.

They asked EVERYONE if they had seen Dish and Spoon.
Even the scary monster in Izzy's closet.

sniff

Where in the universe were Dish and Spoon?

It looked like Dish and Spoon might never return.

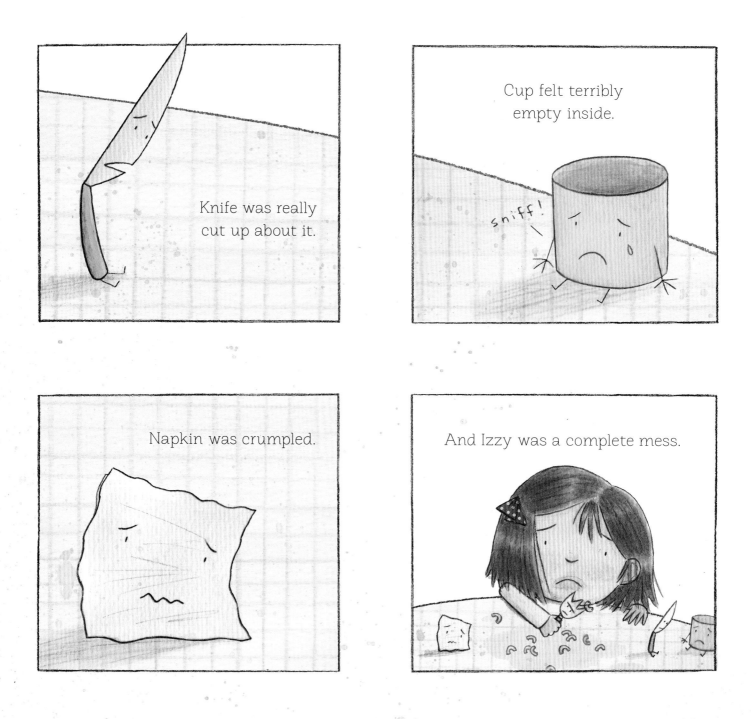

Knife was really cut up about it.

Cup felt terribly empty inside.

Napkin was crumpled.

And Izzy was a complete mess.

But then they got a special delivery.

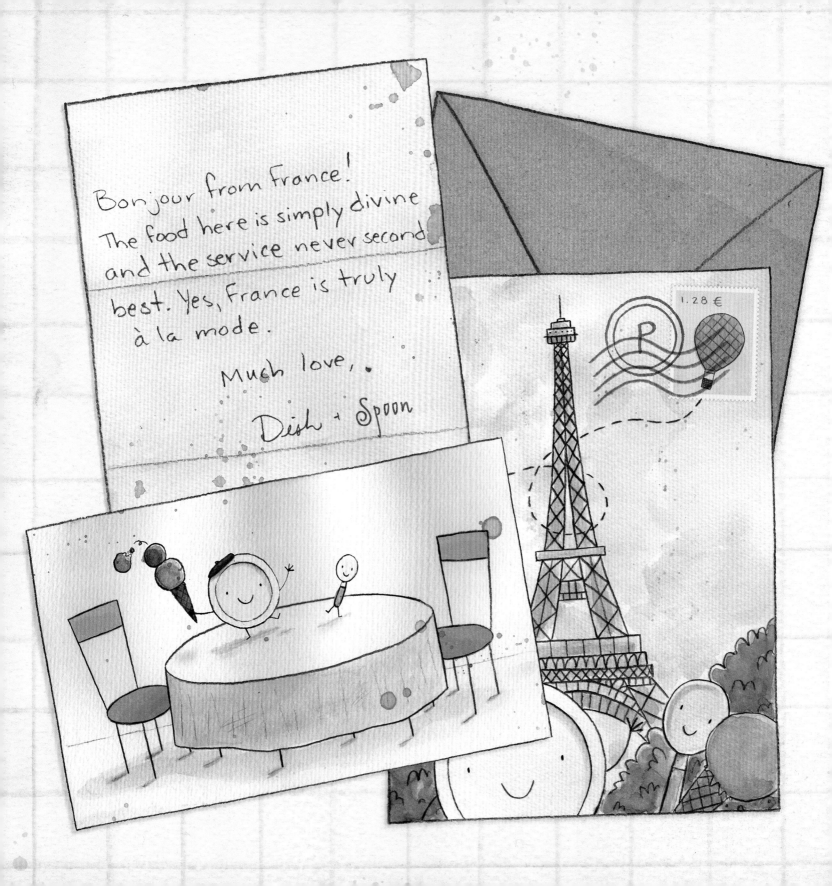

Bonjour from France!
The food here is simply divine
and the service never second
best. Yes, France is truly
à la mode.

Much love,

Dish + Spoon

1.28 €
P

Izzy would have taken off for France right then and there, but her parents didn't understand.

"Don't be absurd! We are NOT going to France," said Mom.

"Very funny, Izzy," said Dad. "And did the cow jump over the moon?"

Not knowing what else to do, Izzy,
Knife, Fork, Cup, and Napkin waited . . .

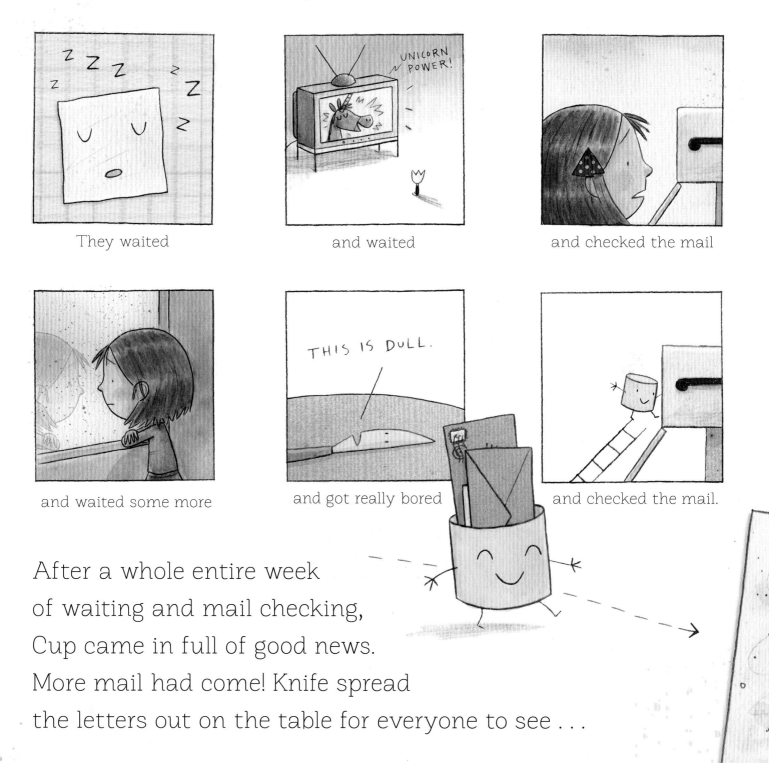

They waited

and waited

and checked the mail

and waited some more

and got really bored

and checked the mail.

After a whole entire week
of waiting and mail checking,
Cup came in full of good news.
More mail had come! Knife spread
the letters out on the table for everyone to see . . .

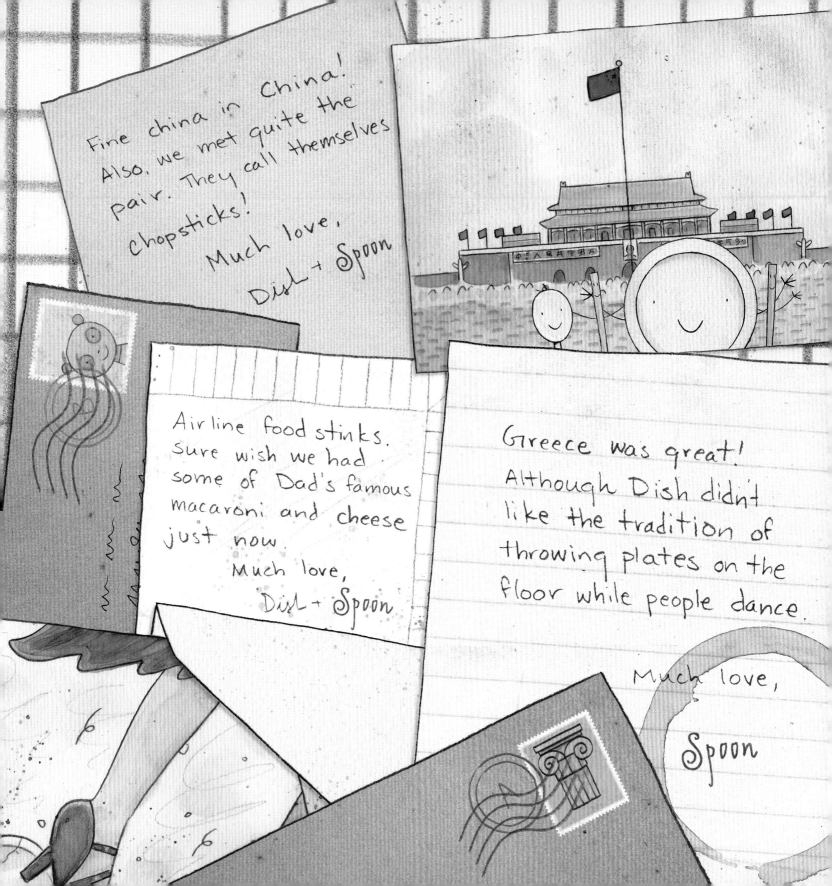

Fine china in China!
Also, we met quite the
pair. They call themselves
chopsticks!
Much love,
Dish + Spoon

Airline food stinks.
Sure wish we had
some of Dad's famous
macaroni and cheese
just now.
Much love,
Dish + Spoon

Greece was great!
Although Dish didn't
like the tradition of
throwing plates on the
floor while people dance.

Much love,
Spoon

All the mail from Dish and Spoon gave Izzy an idea. She would send them a letter! And also some homemade macaroni and cheese.

After some more waiting and lots more mail checking, they got a note back from Spoon.

Dish and Spoon came back to the table just in time for dinner.

The macaroni and cheese was delicious, and everything was set right again.

Yippee!

But then there was a knock (two, actually) on the door.

Ni hao! Dish and Spoon said we should come visit.
Hope you don't mind if we STICK around awhile.